All You Need for a Snowman

Illustrated by

BARBARA LAVALLEE

All You Need for a Snowman

ALICE SCHERTLE

SCHOLASTIC INC.
New York Toronto London Auckland Sydney
Mexico City New Delhi Hong Kong Buenos Aires

ISBN 0-439-58562-7

 Published by Scholastic Inc., 557 Broadway, New York, NY 10012,
by arrangement with Harcourt, Inc.

12 11 10 9 8 7 6 5 4 3 2 1 4 5 6 7 8/0

Printed in the U.S.A. 40

First Scholastic printing, January 2004

The illustrations in this book were done in watercolor and gouache on watercolor paper.

The display type and text type were set in Berling.

Designed by Linda Lockowitz

To Spence and Dylan, pretty good snow men themselves

—A. S.

For Don Conrad, who knows all there is to know about snow

—B. L.

One small snowflake
fluttering down—

that's all you need
for a snowman.

EXCEPT

two more snowflakes...
three flakes... four...

five . . . six . . . seven thousand . . .
eight million more . . .

Billions of snowflakes
piled in a mound,
pat them
and pack them
and roll them
around

into one big ball.

And that's all.

One
big cold
well-rolled
snowflake ball—

that's all you need
for a snowman.

EXCEPT

for a middle-sized ball

and a small one.

On top of that
you need a hat.

A short flat hat or

a
tall
one.

Three hand-packed,
triple-stacked
balls of snow.

Hat on top,
where a hat should go—

that's all you need
for a snowman.

EXCEPT for

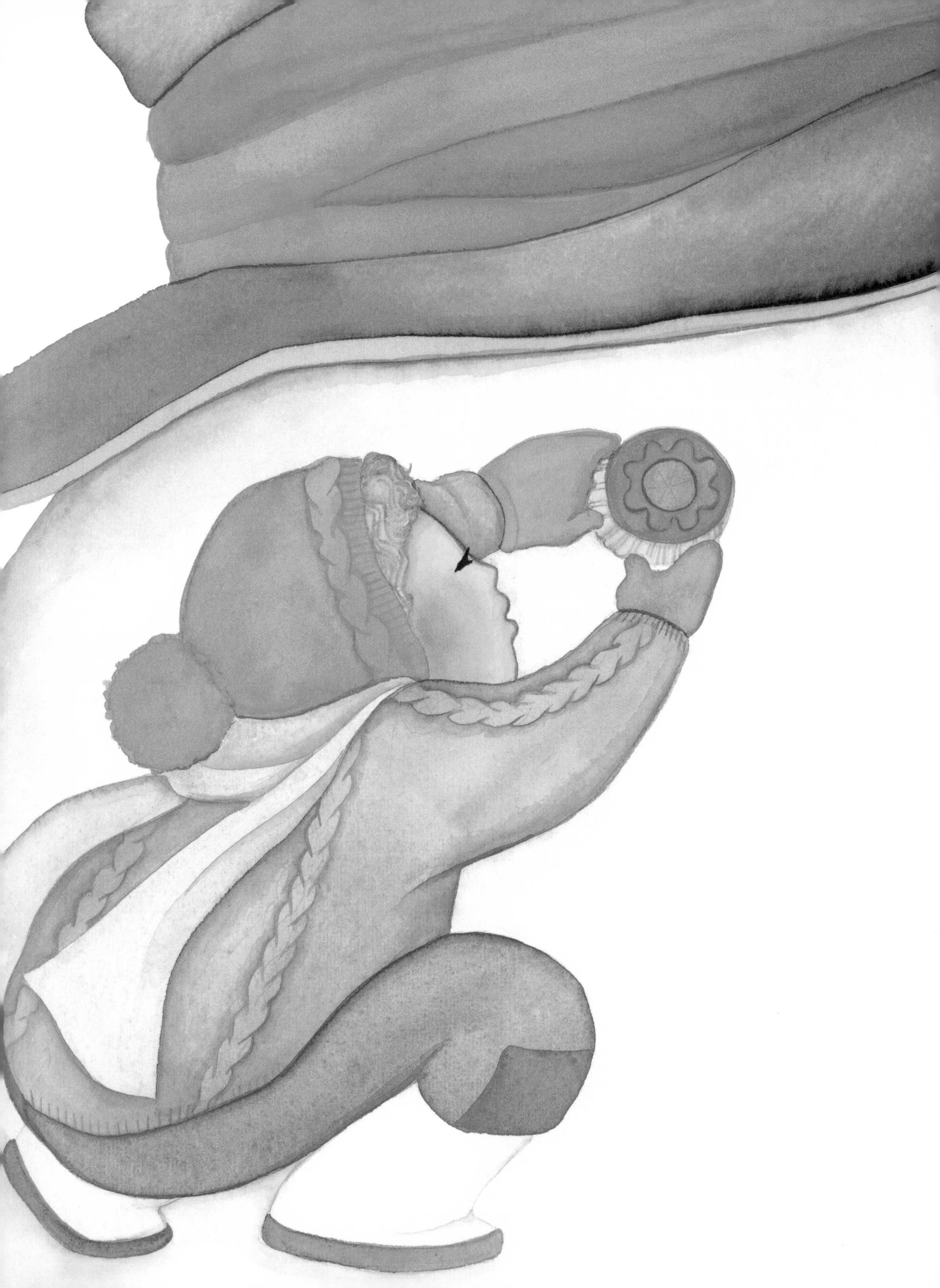

a couple of bottle caps,
round and flat—
stick them under
a snowman's hat.

SURPRISE!
Snowman's eyes!

That's all you need for
a snowman's face.

BUT

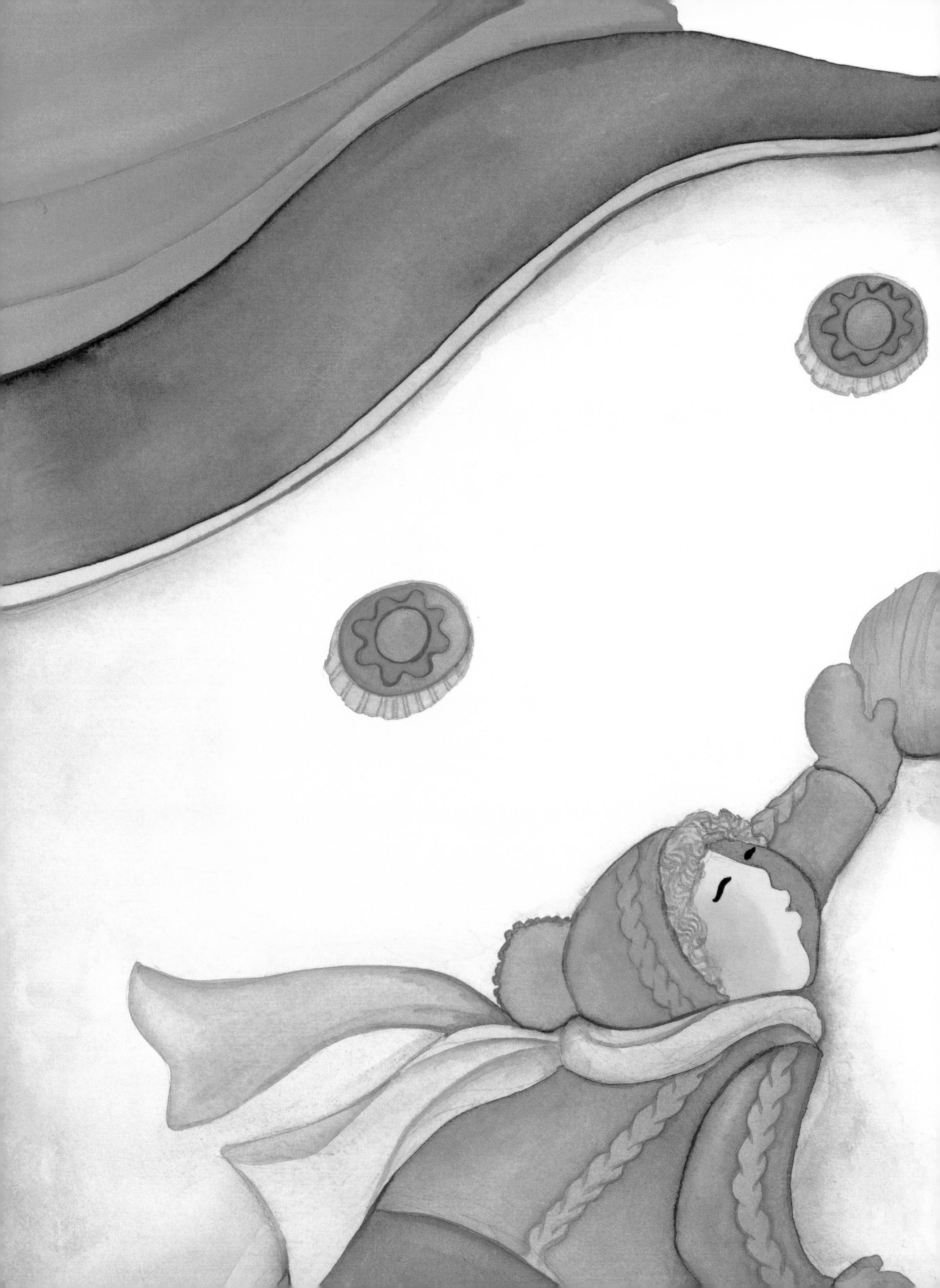

What's in the middle?
An empty space.

That's the place
where the carrot goes

IF

a carrot is
a snowman's
nose.

But what about clothes?

Walnut buttons,
five in a row,
belt in the middle,
boots below,
big wool scarf,
broom to hold,
mittens (in case his hands get cold),
earmuffs,
fanny pack,
something to read—

that's absolutely ALL you need

for a snowman.

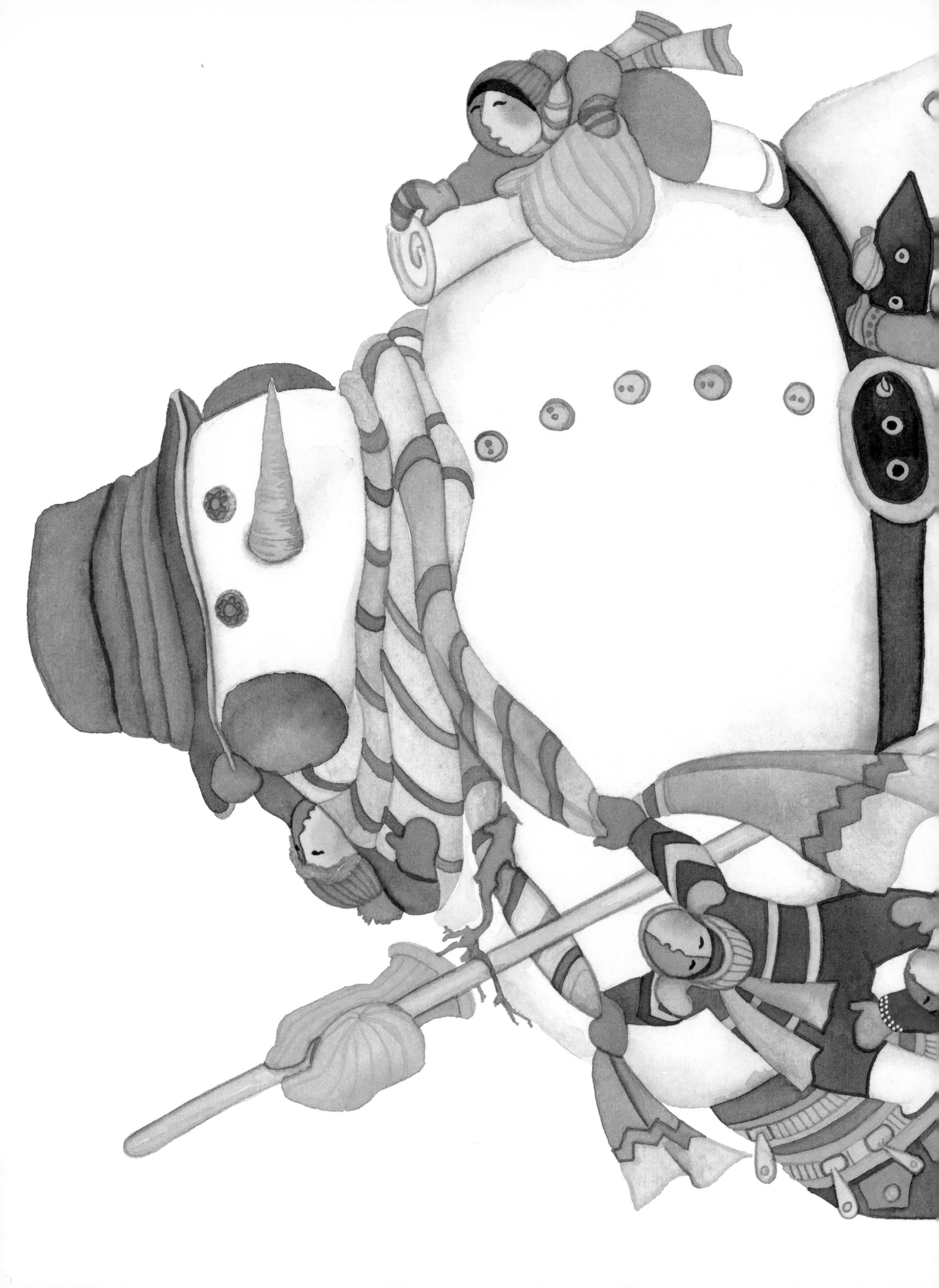

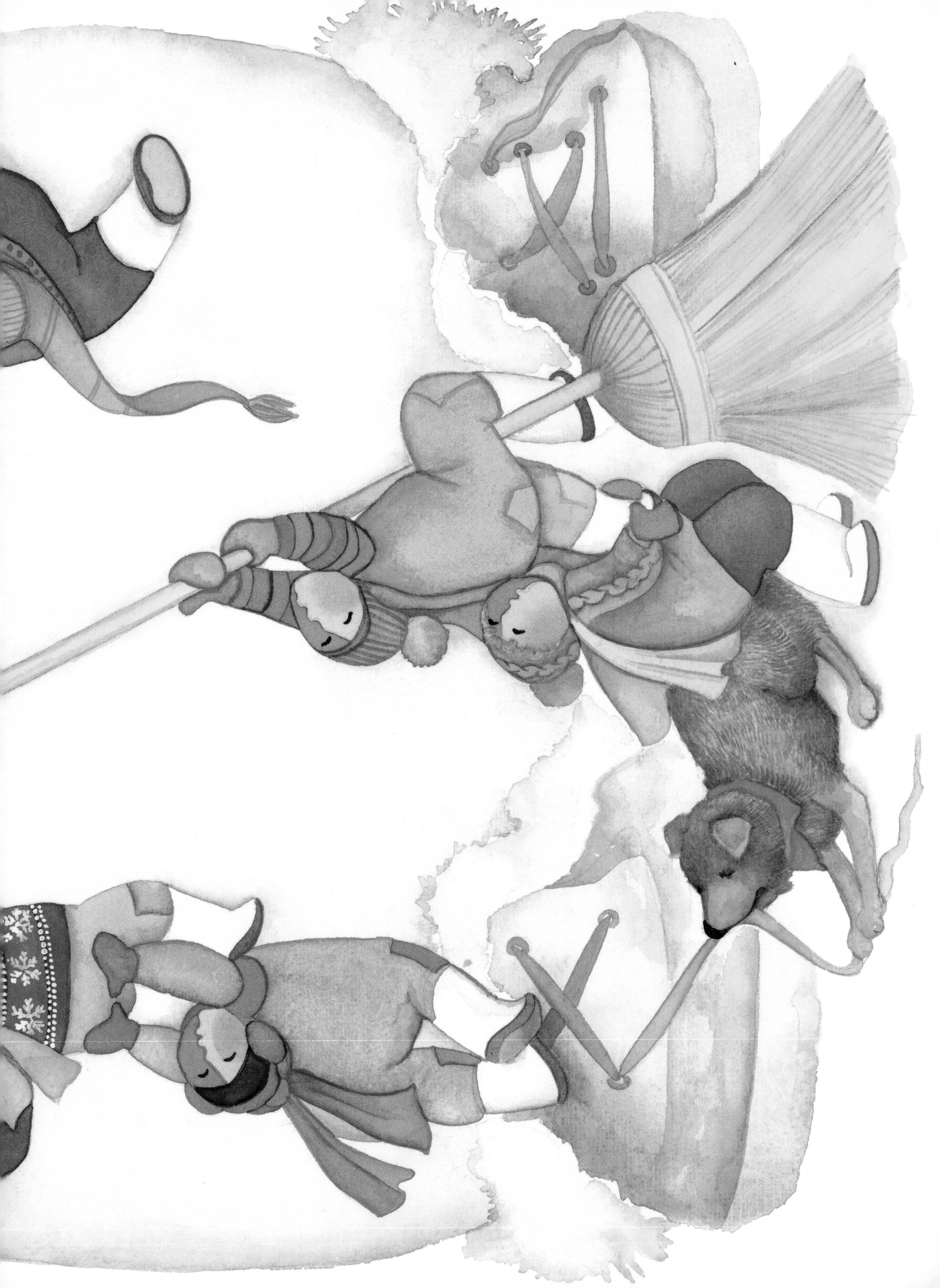

Uh-oh. . . .

Look in the sky again.
One small snowflake falling,

then. . .

soft white snowflakes
filling the sky,

floating down
everywhere,

piling up high…

and THAT'S
all you need

for a snowman's
friend.

The end.